Sweet Dreams

Bedtime Poems, Songs & Lullabies

Bruce Lansky

Illustrated by
Vicki Wehrman

Meadowbrook Press
Distributed by Simon & Schuster
New York

8277592

Library of Congress Cataloging-in-Publication Data
Lansky, Bruce.
        Sweet dreams : bedtime poems, songs & lullabies / written by Bruce Lansky :
illustrated by Vicki Wehrman.
                        p.   cm.
Summary: Original poems and songs for bedtime.
ISBN 0-88166-246-1. – ISBN 0-671-53479-3
1. Children's poetry, American. 2. Children's songs – Texts. 3. Lullabies –Texts.
[1. Bedtime – Poetry. 2. Lullabies. 3. Songs 4. American poetry.]
I. Wehrman, Vicki, ill. II. Title. PS3562.A564S94 1996
811'. 54-dc20   95-25559
                                                              CIP
                                                                  AC

ISBN: 0-88166-229-1
Simon & Schuster Order # 0-671-57046-3

Managing Editor: Dale Howard
Editorial Research: Craig Hansen
Editorial Coordinator: Cathy Broberg
Production Manager: Amy Unger
Graphic Designers: Linda Norton, Erik Broberg

Published by Meadowbrook Press, 18318 Minnetonka Boulevard, Deephaven, MN 55391

BOOK TRADE DISTRIBUTION by Simon & Schuster, a division of Simon and
Schuster, Inc., 1230 Avenue of the Americas, New York, NY 10020.

99 98 97 96   10 9 8 7 6 5 4 3 2 1

Printed in Hong Kong.

⭐ Thank You! ⭐

We loved working with the parents and their children who helped us select the poems, songs, and
lullabies in this collection. Your enthusiasm for this project made it a joyful experience for all of us.
Our reading panel included the families of Sonja Brown, Chris Bruce, Charles Ghigna, Babs Bell
Hajdusiewicz, Julie "Boo" Hanning, Joan and Robert Hursh, Laura Irvin, Jo S. Kittinger, Kim
Koehler, Ann Lynch, Vicki McKinney, Lois Muehl, Lori Reed, Robert Scotellaro, Beverly
Thompson, Esther Towns, Dawn Trappen, Penny Warner, and Julie Zumwalt.

Contents

Bedtime Poems

Bedtime Songs and Lullabies

Good Night, Sun

The sun is setting in the west.
The evening shadows grow.
A bird is flying to it's nest,
so homeward I must go.

The sun has vanished from the sky,
replaced by starry light.
It's time to put my jammies on.
It's time to say good night.

4

Stars Above

I'm glad the stars are overhead
and not beneath my feet,
where I might walk all over them
like pebbles on the street.

I think that it's a lucky thing
the stars are up so high.
It's really fun to look at them
way up there in the sky.

Good Night, Sleepyhead

Take a shower,
brush your teeth,
and then jump into bed.

I'll be up to
tuck you in,
my little sleepyhead.

6

I Love You Sooo Much!

I love you as much
as mice love cheese.
I love you as much
as birds love trees.

I love you as much
as cats love mice.
I love you as much
as cooks love spice.

I love you as much
as frogs love flies.
I love you as much
as kids love pies.

Why do I love you
as much as all that?
Because I'm your parent
and that is that!

One More

One more story,
one more drink.
(That'll give me
time to think.)

One more backrub,
soft and slow;
rub me high and
rub me low.

One more hug and
kiss good-night;
now you can turn
off the light.

One more thing I'd
like to say:
thanks for such a
happy day.

Thanks

Thanks for the story
and thanks for the drink
you brought all the way
from the bathroom sink.
Thanks for the backrub;
I've just one more wish:
a chocolate sundae
with nuts in a dish!

I'm Thankful

I'm thankful for the people
who've helped me through the day:
my parents and my teachers,
the friends with whom I play.
I'm grateful for my food and clothes,
the roof above my head.
And now this little prayer is done,
so I can go to bed.

Snuggle Me

Snuggle me, snuggle me, snuggle me, do.
For a good snuggle, you've got to have two.
Snuggle me, snuggle me, snuggle me, do.
There's no one I'd rather be snuggling than you.

Ready for Sleep

Now I lay me
down to bed.
A fluffy pillow
rests my head.
A woolen blanket
warms my toes.
The smell of pine trees
fills my nose.
The sound of ticking
clocks I hear—
a sign that sleep
is drawing near.
I'm feeling cozy
in my bed,
and soon sweet dreams will
fill my head.

11

Good Night, Night

Good night, birdie.
Good night, fish.
Good night, empty
ice-cream dish.

Good night, twinkling
little stars.
Good night, Venus.
Good night, Mars.

Good night, little
rocking chair.
Good night, cuddly
teddy bear.

Good night, fingers.
Good night, toes.
Good night, eyebrows.
Good night, nose.

Good night, pillow.
Rest my head.
Good night, blanket.
Warm my bed.

Good night, bed lamp.
Good night, light.
Time for sleeping.
Good night, night.

13

Instructions for a Happy Dream

Think of candy.
Think of toys.
Think of happy
girls and boys.

Think of apples.
Think of pears.
Think of cuddly
teddy bears.

Think of dancing
in the rain.
Think of flying
on a plane.

Think of swimming
in a brook.
Think of stories
from a book.

Think of rainbows
in the sky.
Think of ice cream
on a pie.

Think of berries
topped with cream.
Then you'll have a
happy dream.

Think of fingers
full of rings.
Think of all your
favorite things.

15

My Bed Is Like a Sailing Ship

My bed is like a sailing ship—
when I'm tucked in, I take a trip.
I leave behind my busy day
and sail to places far away.

I sail past beaches, gleaming white,
with palm trees swaying in the night.
I watch the waves break on the shore,
and then I see my bedroom floor!

I blink my eyes, I scratch my head—
my ship is home, I'm back in bed.
My ship goes sailing every night
and sails home in the morning light.

Twinkle, Twinkle, Little Star

Twinkle, twinkle, little star,
how I wonder why you are
up above the world so high,
lighting up the evening sky.

Every night, I look to see
if you're shining down on me.
When I see your twinkling light,
then it's time to say, "Good night."

Twinkle, Twinkle, Little Plane

Twinkle, twinkle, little plane,
flying through the pouring rain.
As your colored lights speed by,
they brighten up the cloudy sky.

Flashing lights are on your wings,
so you won't bump into things.
How I hope your trip will be
smooth and safe and trouble-free.

If You're Tired and You Know It

(To the tune of "If You're Happy and You Know It")

If you're dirty and you know it, take a bath.
If you're dirty and you know it, take a bath.
If you're dirty and you know it,
then it's time for you to show it.
If you're dirty and you know it, take a bath.

If it's bedtime and you know it, brush your teeth.
If it's bedtime and you know it, brush your teeth.
If it's bedtime and you know it,
then it's time for you to show it.
If it's bedtime and you know it, brush your teeth.

If you're tired and you know it, go to bed.
If you're tired and you know it, go to bed.
        If you're tired and you know it,
        then it's time for you to show it.
If you're tired and you know it, go to bed.

If you're sleepy and you know it, close your eyes.
If you're sleepy and you know it, close your eyes.
        If you're sleepy and you know it,
        then it's time for you to show it.
If you're sleepy and you know it, close your eyes.

I Love You, Love You, Love You
(To the tune of "Skidamarink")

I love you when it's raining.
I love you when it's dry.
I love you when it's snowing,
and clouds are in the sky.

Chorus:
Skidamarink-a-dink-a-dink,
skidamarink-a-doo;
I love you.
Skidamarink-a-dink-a-dink,
skidamarink-a-doo;
yes, I do.

I love you when it's freezing.
I love you when it's hot.
I love you when it's foggy.
I love you when it's not.

I love you when you're grumpy.
I love you when you're sad.
I love you when you're silly,
and even when you're mad.

I love you in the morning.
I love you late at night.
I love you when it's bedtime,
and when we kiss good-night.

I love you, love you, love you,
I love you, yes, I do.
The reason that I love you—
I love you 'cause you're you.

23

I'll Always Love You

(To the tune of "My Bonnie Lies over the Ocean")

Forever and ever I'll love you,
whatever you say or you do.
I promise I'll always forgive you.
I promise I'll always love you.

Chorus:
Always…
love you…
no matter whatever you say or do.
Always…
love you…
I will always love you.

You might forget all of your manners.
You might leave your room in a mess.
I promise I'll always forgive you.
I won't love you any the less.

You might spill your milk on the table.
You might eat up all of the fudge.
I promise I'll always forgive you.
I never will carry a grudge.

You might be a grouch in the morning.
You might wake me up late at night.
I promise I'll always forgive you.
I'll hug you and make it all right.

25

The Bedtime Song

(To the tune of "Frère Jacques")

It's your bedtime.
It's your bedtime.
Brush your teeth.
Brush your teeth.
Put on your pajamas.
Put on your pajamas.
Jump in bed.
Jump in bed.

Time for sleeping.
Time for sleeping.
Say your prayers.
Say your prayers.
Give me a good-night kiss.
Give me a good-night kiss.
Close your eyes.
Close your eyes.

Melody of Love

(To the tune of "Brahms' Lullaby")

I will sing you a song.
Close your eyes now and listen.
I will sing you to sleep
with a melody of love.

I love you, yes, I do.
May your sweet dreams come true.
I love you, yes, I do.
May your sweet dreams come true.

27

Good Night, Sweetie

(To the tune of "Good Night, Ladies")

Good night, sweetie.
Good night, sweetie.
Good night, sweetie,
it's time to go to bed.

Now it's time to go to bed,
go to bed, go to bed.
Now it's time to go to bed.
It's time to go to bed.

Sleep tight, sweetie.
Sleep tight, sweetie.
Sleep tight, sweetie,
it's time to close your eyes.

Now it's time to close your eyes,
close your eyes, close your eyes.
Now it's time to close your eyes.
It's time to close your eyes.

Sweet dreams, sweetie.
Sweet dreams, sweetie.
Sweet dreams, sweetie,
it's time to fall asleep.

Now it's time to fall asleep,
fall asleep, fall asleep.
Now it's time to fall asleep.
It's time to fall asleep.

28

Good Night, Sleep Tight

(To the tune of "Good Night, Irene")

Puppies sleep on carpets.
Fishes sleep in brooks.
Kittens sleep on sofas.
Chipmunks sleep in nooks.

Chorus:
Good night, sleep tight.
Good night, sleep tight.
I love you so,
and I hate to go—
but it's time to say, "Good night."

Honeybees sleep in beehives.
Piggies sleep in pens.
Horses sleep in stables,
and bears sleep in their dens.

Would you like to sleep in a pigpen?
Would you like to sleep in a brook?
Would you like to sleep in your own warm bed,
after reading your favorite book?

30

Rock-a-Bye, Baby

Rock-a-bye, baby, on the treetop.
When the wind blows, the cradle will rock;
when the birds sing, the baby will smile,
and fall asleep happy in a short while.

31

Hush, Little Darling

(To the tune of "Hush, Little Baby")

Hush, little darling, don't you cry.
Mama's gonna sing you a lullaby.

And when that lullaby is through,
Mama's gonna stay right here with you.

And if you wake up in the night,
Mama's gonna make everything all right.

Hush, little darling, don't you weep.
Mama's gonna stay here until you sleep.

32